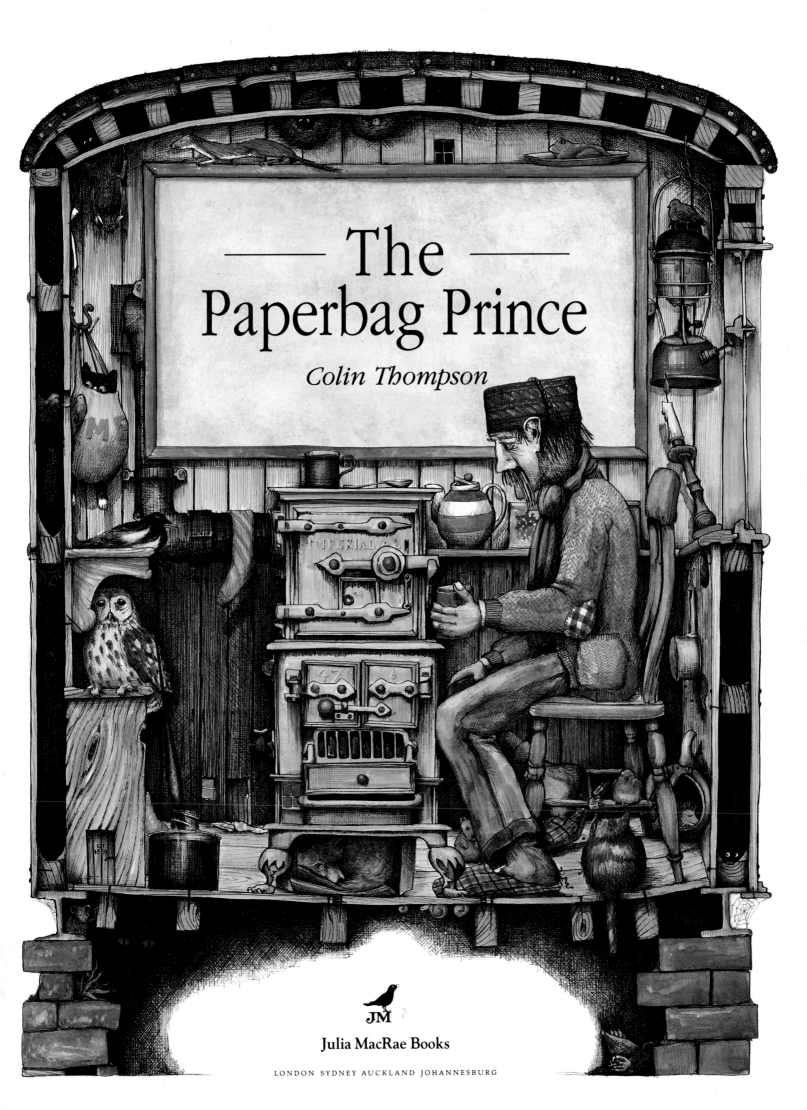

The Paperbag Prince

Colin Thompson

Julia MacRae Books

LONDON SYDNEY AUCKLAND JOHANNESBURG

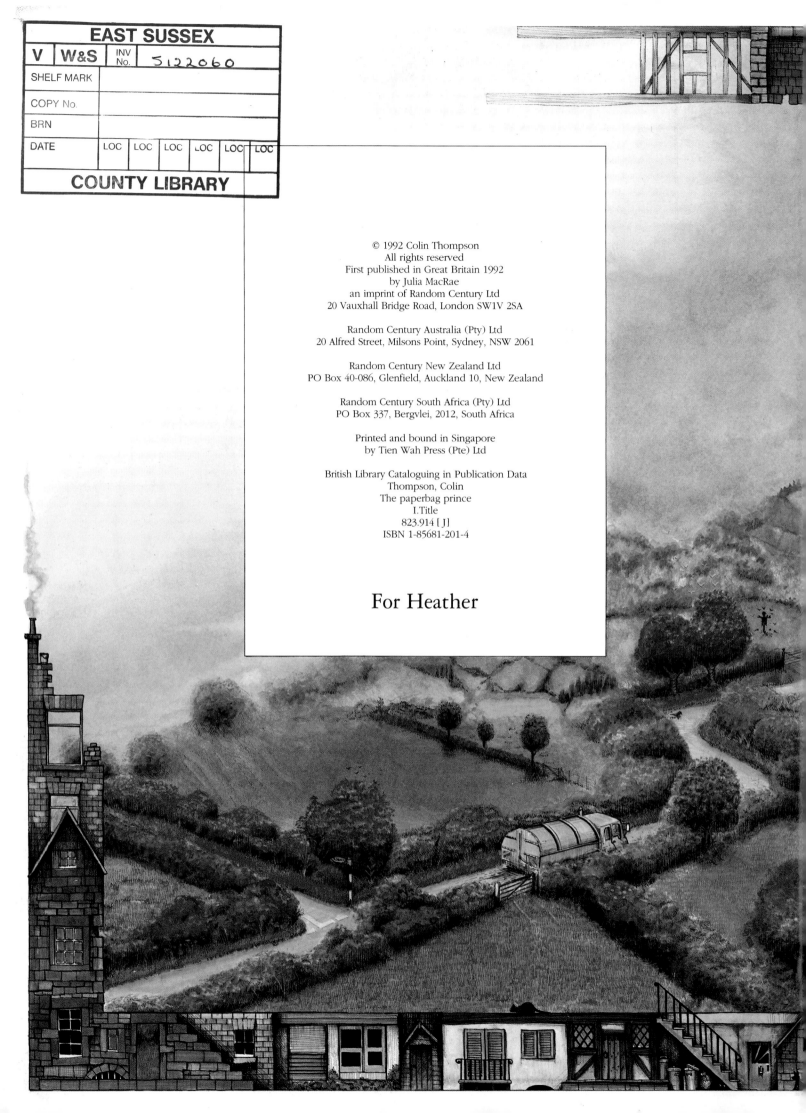

© 1992 Colin Thompson
All rights reserved
First published in Great Britain 1992
by Julia MacRae
an imprint of Random Century Ltd
20 Vauxhall Bridge Road, London SW1V 2SA

Random Century Australia (Pty) Ltd
20 Alfred Street, Milsons Point, Sydney, NSW 2061

Random Century New Zealand Ltd
PO Box 40-086, Glenfield, Auckland 10, New Zealand

Random Century South Africa (Pty) Ltd
PO Box 337, Bergvlei, 2012, South Africa

Printed and bound in Singapore
by Tien Wah Press (Pte) Ltd

British Library Cataloguing in Publication Data
Thompson, Colin
The paperbag prince
I.Title
823.914 [J]
ISBN 1-85681-201-4

For Heather

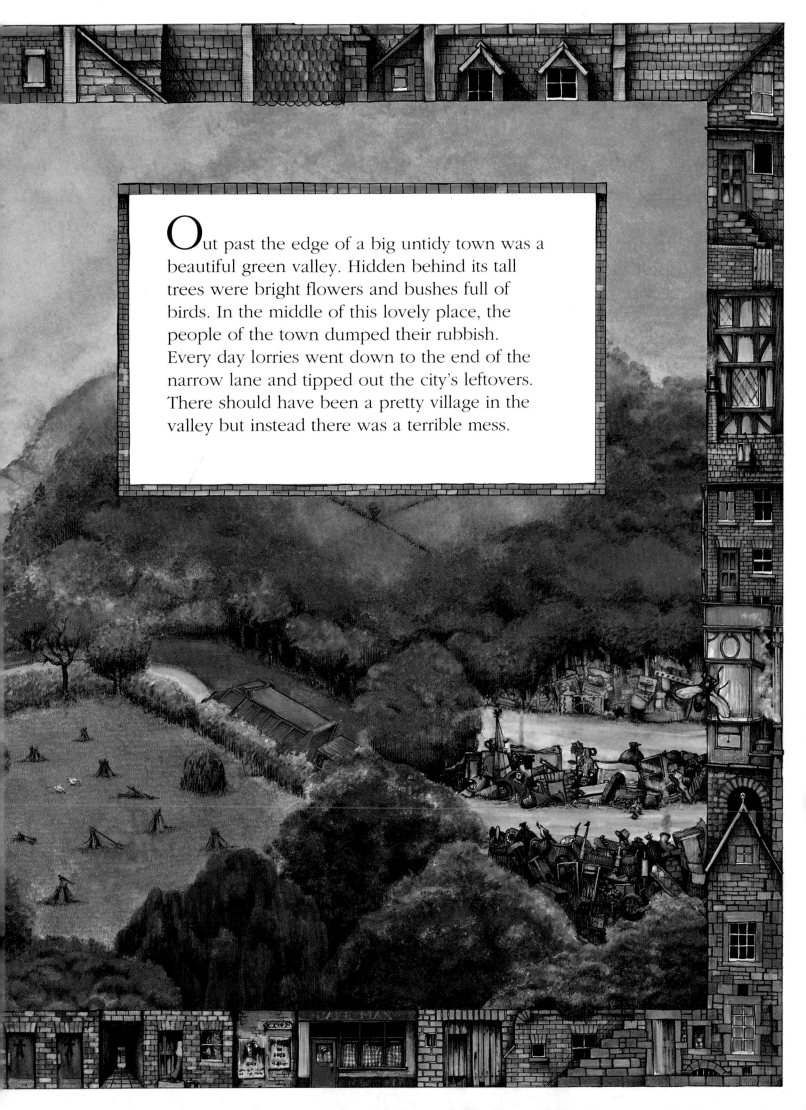

Out past the edge of a big untidy town was a beautiful green valley. Hidden behind its tall trees were bright flowers and bushes full of birds. In the middle of this lovely place, the people of the town dumped their rubbish. Every day lorries went down to the end of the narrow lane and tipped out the city's leftovers. There should have been a pretty village in the valley but instead there was a terrible mess.

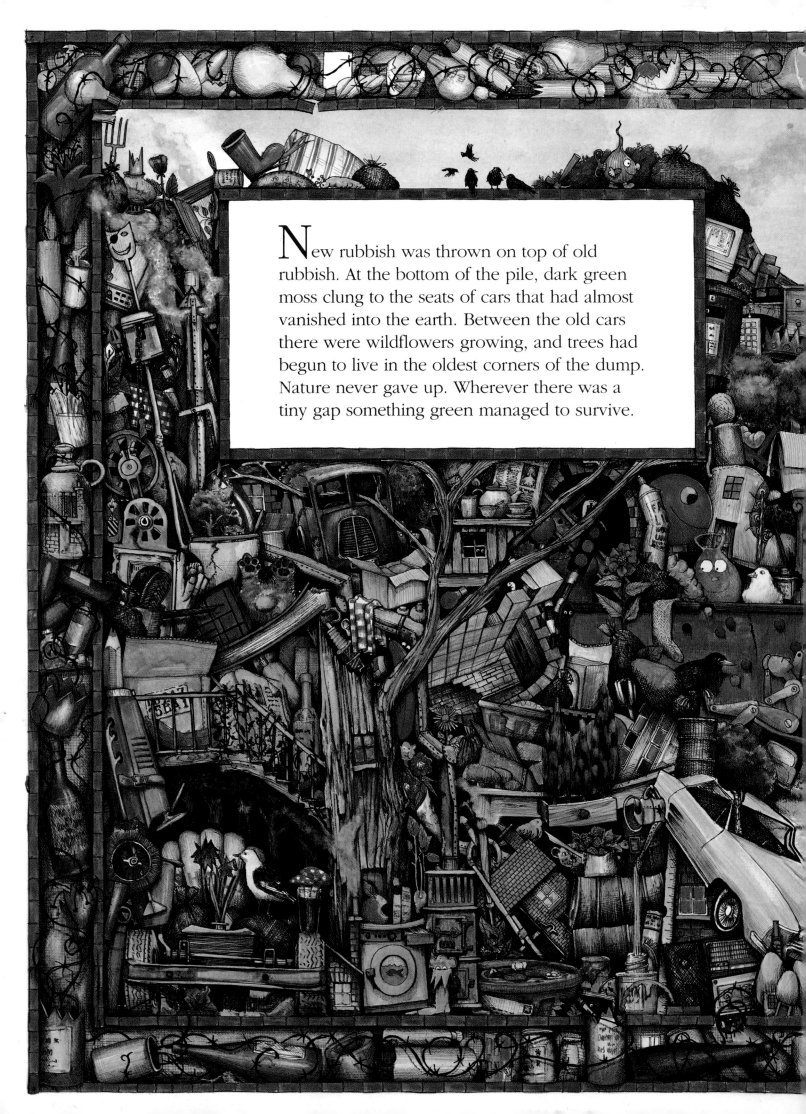

New rubbish was thrown on top of old rubbish. At the bottom of the pile, dark green moss clung to the seats of cars that had almost vanished into the earth. Between the old cars there were wildflowers growing, and trees had begun to live in the oldest corners of the dump. Nature never gave up. Wherever there was a tiny gap something green managed to survive.

Animals lived there too, not just mice and insects but larger creatures like cats and weasels and foxes. For them it was a wonderful place, safe from the attentions of Man. The twisted, torn bodies of refrigerators, pressing into the flattened frames of old beds, made a hundred little corridors and highways. Under an old clock lazy dormice slept. Inside a television a family of sparrows made their home. There was life everywhere. Even in a tiny puddle in a worn-out shoe there were mosquito larvae watching for summer.

Humans didn't like to be near the rubbish. For them it was a dangerous place, with rusty metal and broken glass and rotting things that smelt of disease. In a back corner there was the Poison Pool where large metal drums leaked into a brown pond and nothing, not even the smallest plant, could live. The animals were cleverer than Man. They kept away from the Poison Pool and thrived in their man-made environment.

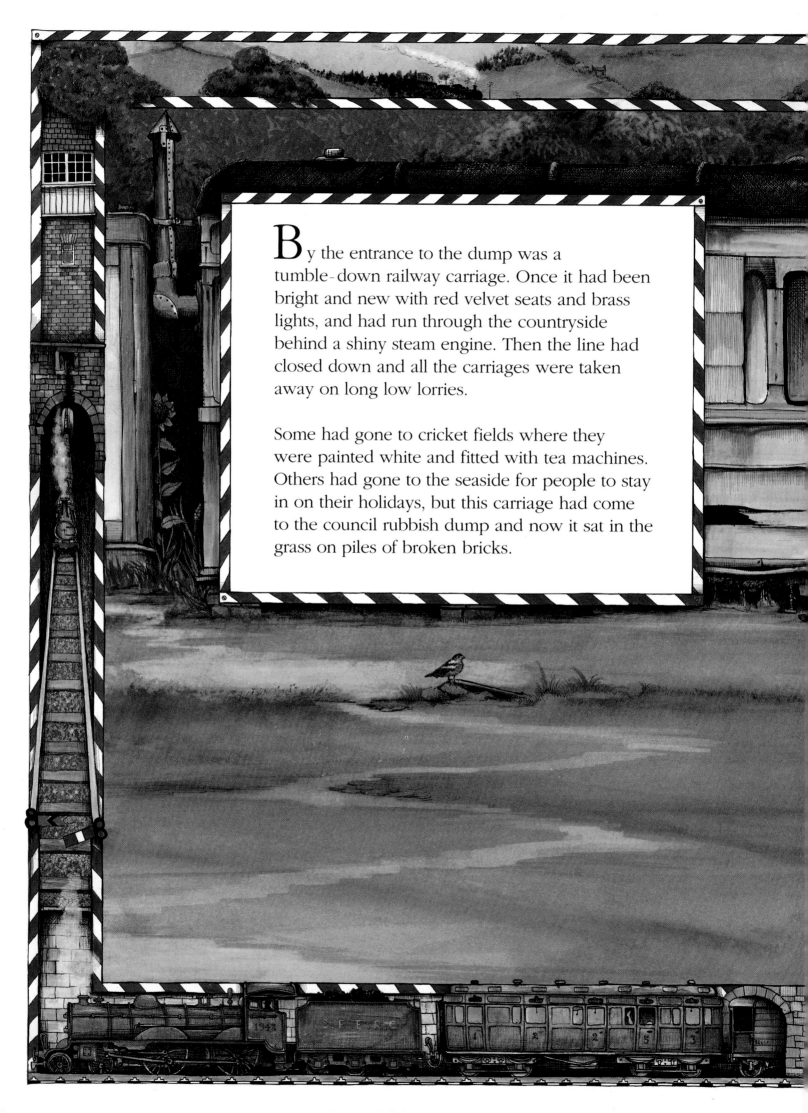

By the entrance to the dump was a
tumble-down railway carriage. Once it had been
bright and new with red velvet seats and brass
lights, and had run through the countryside
behind a shiny steam engine. Then the line had
closed down and all the carriages were taken
away on long low lorries.

Some had gone to cricket fields where they
were painted white and fitted with tea machines.
Others had gone to the seaside for people to stay
in on their holidays, but this carriage had come
to the council rubbish dump and now it sat in the
grass on piles of broken bricks.

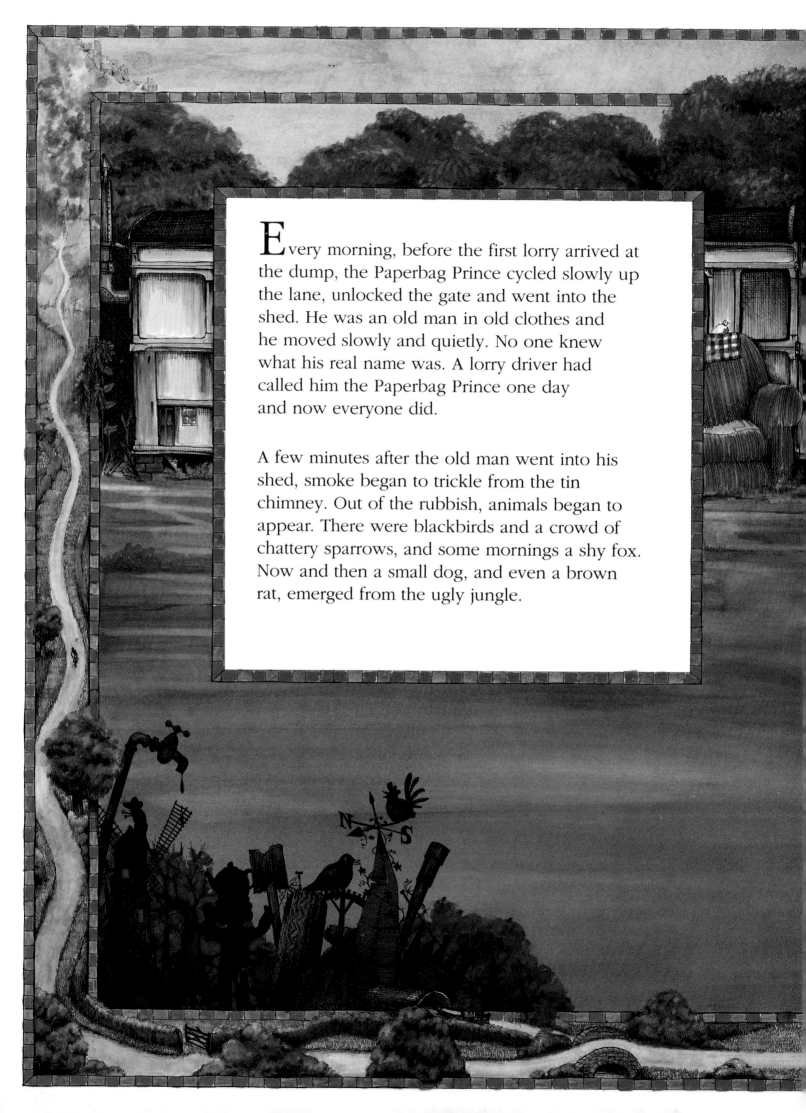

Every morning, before the first lorry arrived at the dump, the Paperbag Prince cycled slowly up the lane, unlocked the gate and went into the shed. He was an old man in old clothes and he moved slowly and quietly. No one knew what his real name was. A lorry driver had called him the Paperbag Prince one day and now everyone did.

A few minutes after the old man went into his shed, smoke began to trickle from the tin chimney. Out of the rubbish, animals began to appear. There were blackbirds and a crowd of chattery sparrows, and some mornings a shy fox. Now and then a small dog, and even a brown rat, emerged from the ugly jungle.

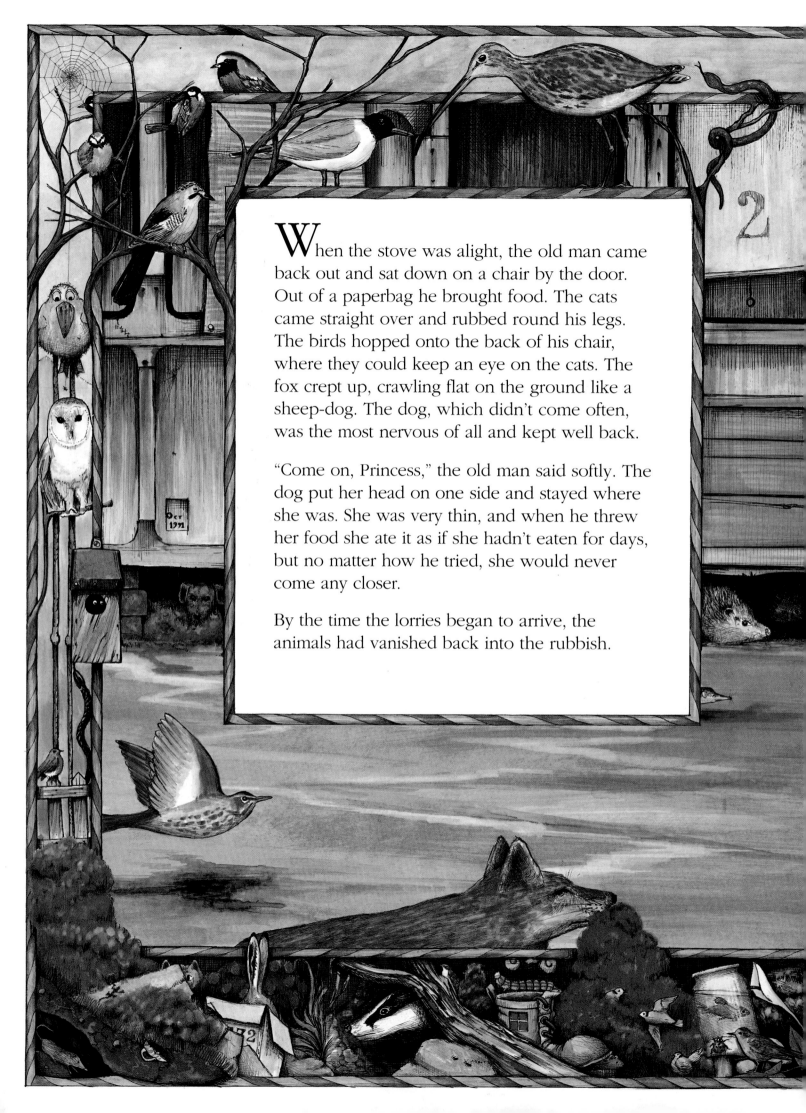

When the stove was alight, the old man came back out and sat down on a chair by the door. Out of a paperbag he brought food. The cats came straight over and rubbed round his legs. The birds hopped onto the back of his chair, where they could keep an eye on the cats. The fox crept up, crawling flat on the ground like a sheep-dog. The dog, which didn't come often, was the most nervous of all and kept well back.

"Come on, Princess," the old man said softly. The dog put her head on one side and stayed where she was. She was very thin, and when he threw her food she ate it as if she hadn't eaten for days, but no matter how he tried, she would never come any closer.

By the time the lorries began to arrive, the animals had vanished back into the rubbish.

All day long lorries came, tipping black bags and broken bits of houses into untidy piles. Seagulls gathered to fight and flap over the mountains of new bags.

The old man poked through everything. He collected wood for his stove and old clothes to wear. He smoothed out old paperbags and piled them up inside wardrobes. Next to his shed there were twelve wardrobes all jammed tight with thousands of paperbags. That was how he got his name.

People seemed to throw stuff away for no reason at all. His carriage was full of last year's radios and beautiful coloured bottles. He had eighty-seven odd shoes, fourteen video recorders, and nineteen television sets, but he had no electricity nor any wish for it.

One day the lorries stopped coming.

The Paperbag Prince sat on his seat in the summer sunshine. A skylark was singing high in the air above him and along the lane it was silent. There was no thundery rumble of heavy lorries approaching. There was nothing, just the skylark. It was wonderful.

"Perhaps it's a holiday," he said to no one in particular, but it wasn't. He leaned back in his chair with his face tipped up towards the warm sun, and was soon fast asleep.

At lunchtime someone shook him awake.

"Hello," said a young lady.

"What? Eh?" said the man, coming back to life. "Who are you?"

"I'm Sarah. I'm from the council."

"Where are the lorries?" asked the old man.

"That's why I'm here," said Sarah. She spoke loudly and slowly as if the old man was an idiot.

"There's no need to shout. I'm not an idiot."

"Of course you're not," Sarah shouted. "The rubbish dump's been closed. We're going to burn all the rubbish in a new machine."

At last, thought the old man and said, "What about this place?"

"It's yours again," said Sarah, handing him some papers. "The council don't need it any more. You can have it back."

As the car drove off, the Paperbag Prince stood there with a big grin on his face. It had been over forty years since his farmhouse had burnt down and they'd taken over his farm for a rubbish dump. They had put him in a council house and paid him quite a lot of money, and every day since then he had come back and watched his land suffer. Now it was all over.

His back stopped aching, and his eyes grew bright as he felt a great weary weight lift from his shoulders. In three weeks' time he would be seventy but in his heart he was twenty-five again. He locked the gate and did a little dance on the tired earth.

His heart sang and must have filled the air with his happiness because one by one his animal friends came out of the dump and watched him. Even the little dog peered out from the shadows of a dustbin.

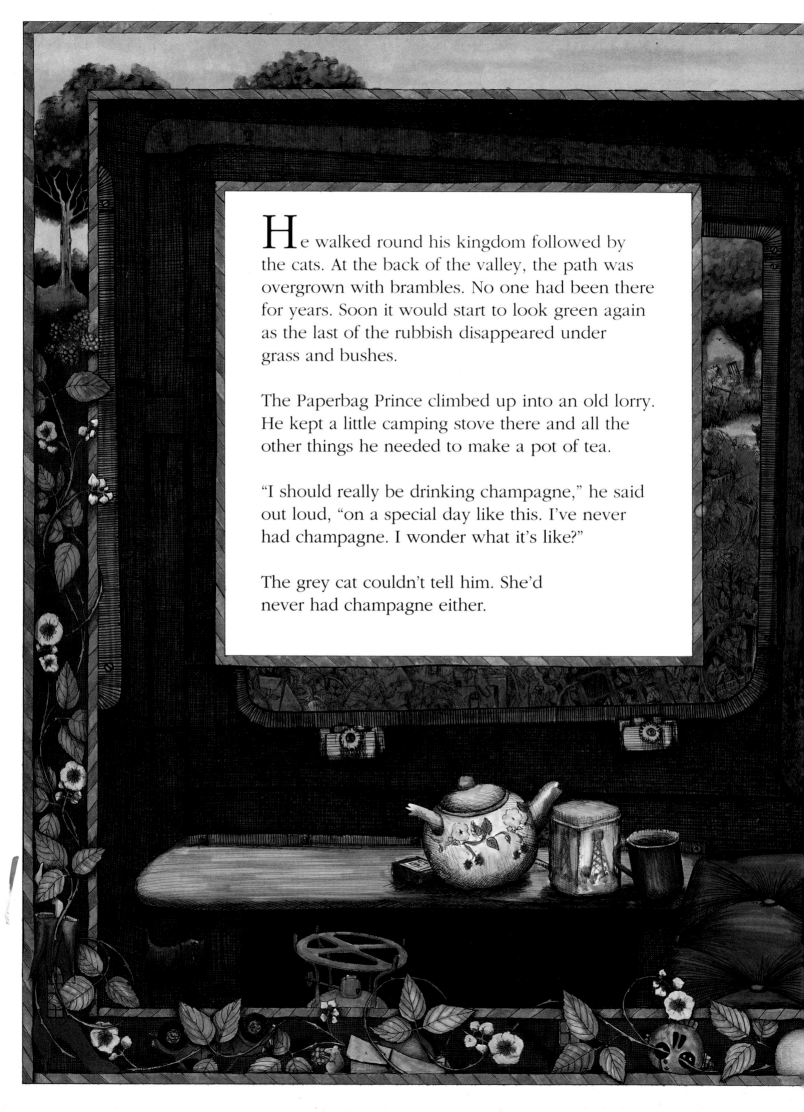

He walked round his kingdom followed by
the cats. At the back of the valley, the path was
overgrown with brambles. No one had been there
for years. Soon it would start to look green again
as the last of the rubbish disappeared under
grass and bushes.

The Paperbag Prince climbed up into an old lorry.
He kept a little camping stove there and all the
other things he needed to make a pot of tea.

"I should really be drinking champagne," he said
out loud, "on a special day like this. I've never
had champagne. I wonder what it's like?"

The grey cat couldn't tell him. She'd
never had champagne either.

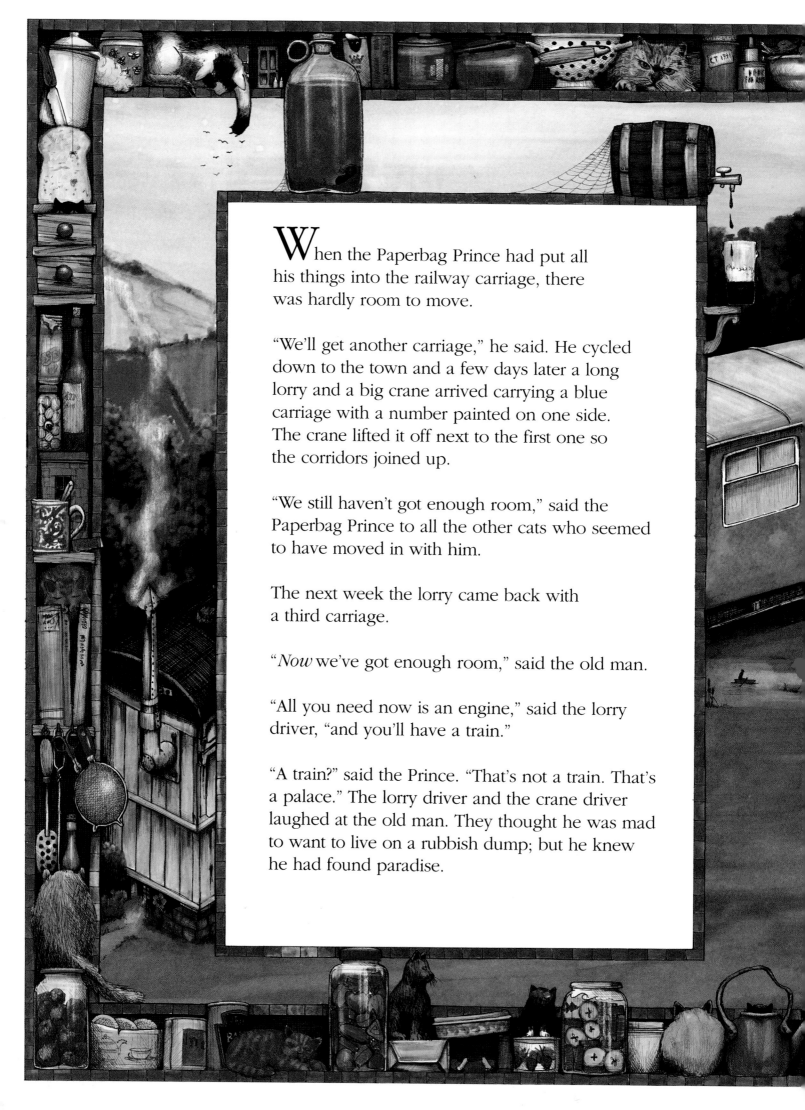

When the Paperbag Prince had put all his things into the railway carriage, there was hardly room to move.

"We'll get another carriage," he said. He cycled down to the town and a few days later a long lorry and a big crane arrived carrying a blue carriage with a number painted on one side. The crane lifted it off next to the first one so the corridors joined up.

"We still haven't got enough room," said the Paperbag Prince to all the other cats who seemed to have moved in with him.

The next week the lorry came back with a third carriage.

"*Now* we've got enough room," said the old man.

"All you need now is an engine," said the lorry driver, "and you'll have a train."

"A train?" said the Prince. "That's not a train. That's a palace." The lorry driver and the crane driver laughed at the old man. They thought he was mad to want to live on a rubbish dump; but he knew he had found paradise.

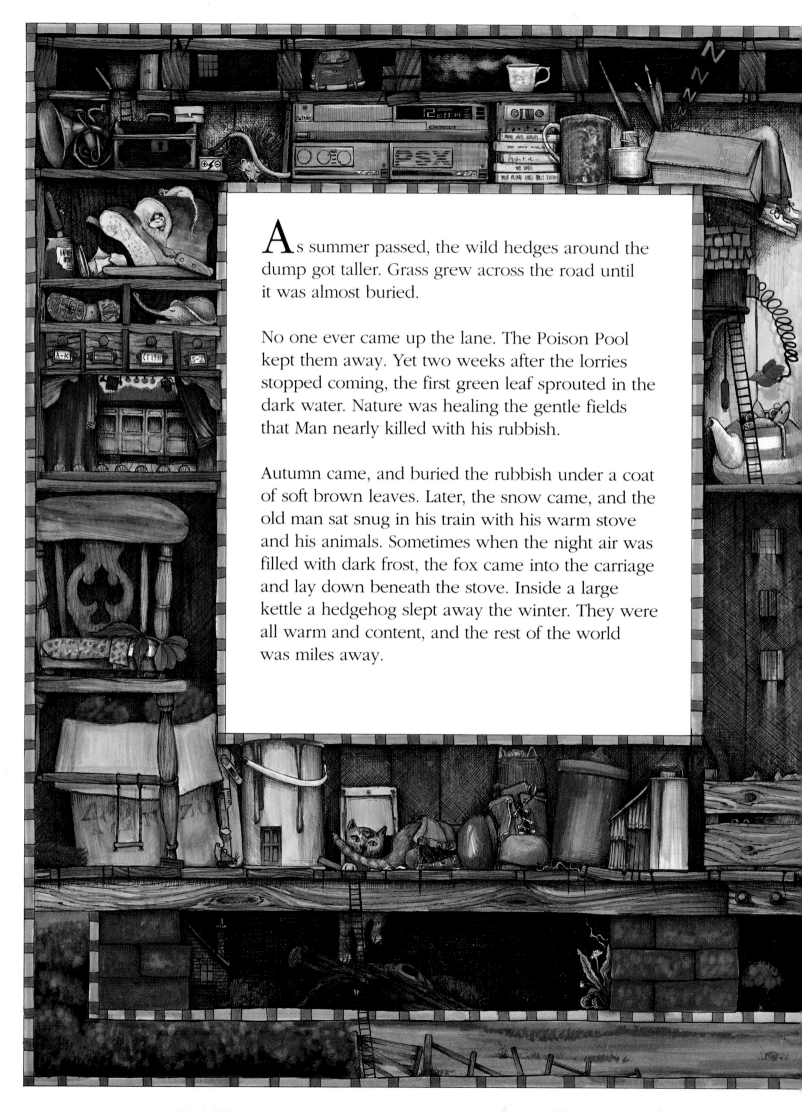

As summer passed, the wild hedges around the dump got taller. Grass grew across the road until it was almost buried.

No one ever came up the lane. The Poison Pool kept them away. Yet two weeks after the lorries stopped coming, the first green leaf sprouted in the dark water. Nature was healing the gentle fields that Man nearly killed with his rubbish.

Autumn came, and buried the rubbish under a coat of soft brown leaves. Later, the snow came, and the old man sat snug in his train with his warm stove and his animals. Sometimes when the night air was filled with dark frost, the fox came into the carriage and lay down beneath the stove. Inside a large kettle a hedgehog slept away the winter. They were all warm and content, and the rest of the world was miles away.

The days got shorter and shorter. It was nearly Christmas. The old man walked through the trees towards the old lorry. He had forgotten to shut the cab door and the seats were covered with snow. As he climbed in to brush it out, something jumped up out of a pile of leaves. It was the little dog. With no new rubbish to scavenge through she had grown even thinner, and was too weak to run away.

"Come on, Princess," said the old man, "there's no need to be afraid."

He put her inside his coat and carried her back home. He fed her and brushed her and tucked her up in his bed. More snow fell during the night, but in the morning the sky was blue from side to side, and the thin sun shone down on the best Christmas the Paperbag Prince and the little dog had ever known.